Walking Home Alone

by Ginger Baker
illustrated by Pamela R. Levy

Richard C. Owen Publishers, Inc.
Katonah, New York

Roberto's older brother went home from school with a bad cold. Now Roberto had to walk home alone and he was afraid.

His older brother had told him, "You can do it, Roberto. You know the way. We walk it every day. Don't worry, you'll be okay."

Roberto did not feel okay.
What if he turned at the wrong corner?
What if he got lost and his family couldn't find him?
What if a big, scary dog chased him?
Roberto did not want to walk home alone.

His teacher said, "Don't worry.
You will do just fine, Roberto.
You know the way home.
You walk it every day."

Roberto began to walk home.

On the way he saw his brother's best friend, Brent.
"Hi, Brent," said Roberto. "I'm walking home
alone today."

Brent said, "I'm walking home alone, too.
I'll walk with you."

Roberto and Brent talked as they walked.

Roberto saw his mama's friend, Mrs. Sosa.
"Hi, Mrs. Sosa," said Roberto. "I'm walking home alone today."

Mrs. Sosa said, "You'll do fine.
May I walk with you? I'm alone, too."

Roberto, Brent, and Mrs. Sosa
talked as they walked.

When they came to the corner,
Roberto saw his friend,
Mr. Brown, the mail carrier.

"Hi, Mr. Brown," said Roberto.
"I'm walking home alone today."

Mr. Brown smiled and said,
"I'd like to walk with you. I'm alone, too."

Roberto, Brent, Mrs. Sosa, and Mr. Brown
talked as they walked.

When they got to Brent's house,
Brent waved goodbye.

"Tell your brother I'll call him tonight,"
he said.

When they got to Mrs. Sosa's house,
Mrs. Sosa said, "Say hello to your mama, Roberto."

Then she waved goodbye.

When they got to Roberto's house,
Mr. Brown put the mail in the mailbox.

"Thanks for walking with me, Roberto,"
he said.

Then he said goodbye.

"I did it!" Roberto said.

He opened the door and called out,
"I'm home! I walked home alone
and I did just fine!"